Milly and Molly

For my grandchildren
Thomas, Harry, Ella and Madeleine

Part of the proceeds from the sale of this book goes to The Friends of Milly, Molly Inc., a charity, which aims to promote the acceptance of diversity and the learning of life skills through literacy - *'for every child, a book.'*

Milly, Molly and Henry

Copyright © MM House Publishing, 2003

Gill Pittar and Cris Morrell assert the moral right to be recognised as the author and illustrator of this work.

Published by
MM House Publishing
P O Box 539
Gisborne, New Zealand
email: books@millymolly.com

Printed by Rhythm Consolidated Berhad, Malaysia

ISBN: 1-86972-030-X

10 9 8 7 6 5 4 3 2 1

Milly, Molly

and

Henry

"We may look different but we feel the same."

What is it about Henry?
Henry knows how he feels and he owns
his feelings.

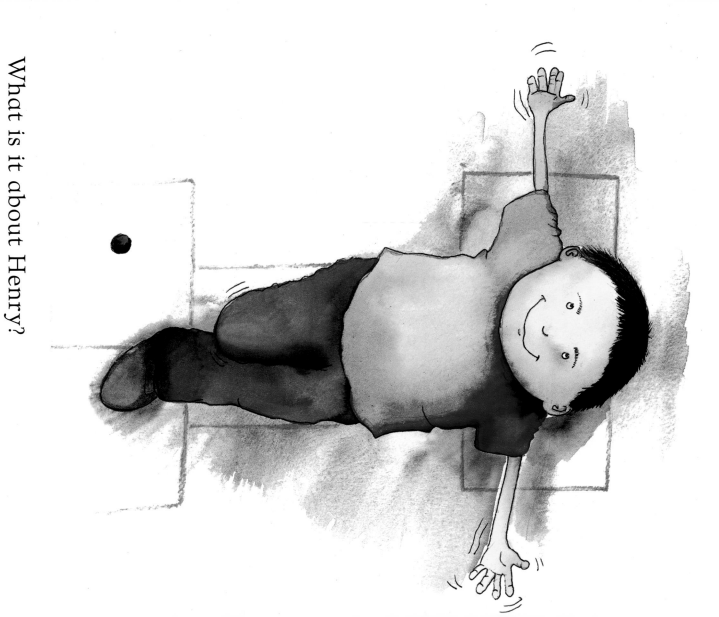

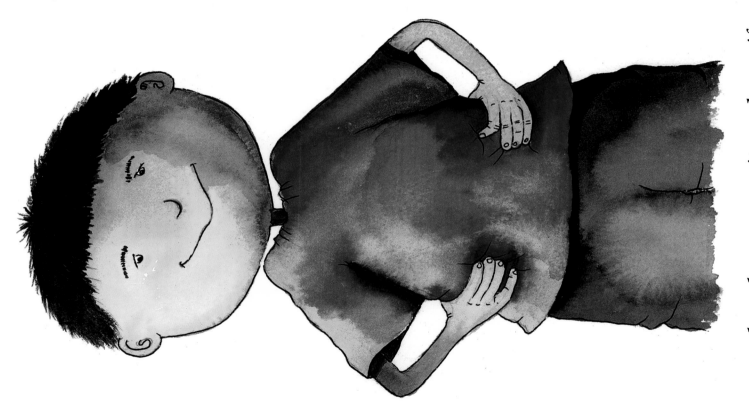

He says no when he means it and yes if it pleases him.

Henry is kind to the girls and nice to the boys.

4

He doesn't blush and he doesn't giggle either.

Henry isn't pushy nor is he backward.

He knows what he likes and what he doesn't.

He doesn't always need a friend to play with

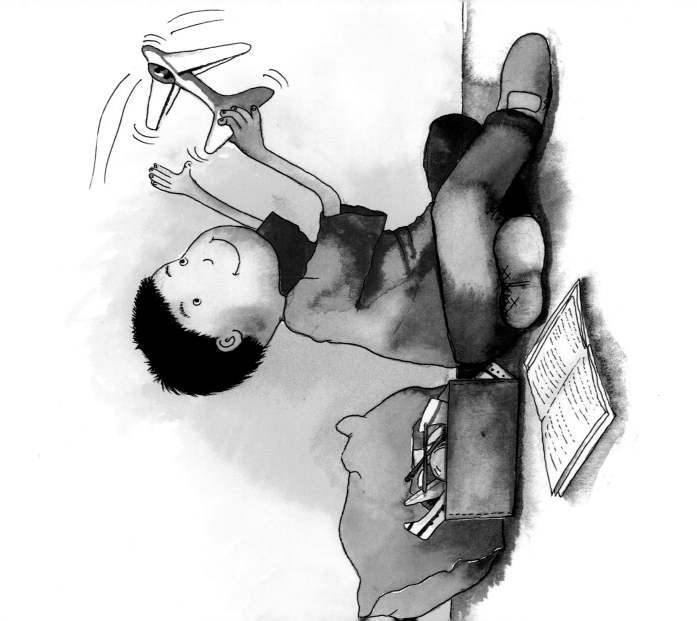

or a soul to talk to.

He laughs loudly at the funny parts

and cries openly through the sad bits.

Reading to the class is a breeze

and making mistakes not a problem.

Henry takes math in his stride

and plays catch one handed.

He doesn't mind being laughed at

or teased and poked fun at.

Henry opens doors for the mothers and stands up for the fathers.

18

He remembers his pleases and never forgets his thank-yous.

Henry owns up to his shortcomings and confesses to his weaknesses.

Henry wears his hair straight when everyone spikes it.

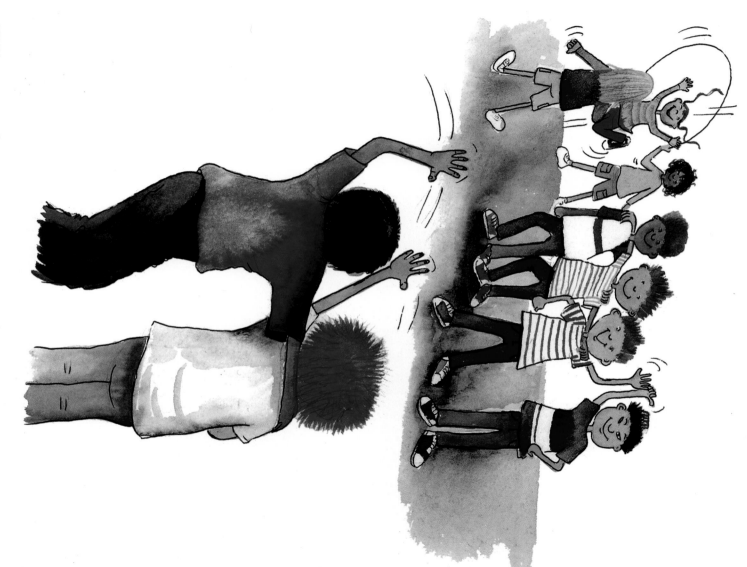

When tight pants are cool, Henry wears baggies.

When blue shirts are in, Henry wears red ones. And who is the most sought-after friend in the school?

Henry!
Henry is Henry and that's all there is to it.

24

Milly, Molly and Henry

The value implicitly expressed in this story is 'self-acceptance' – accepting and being happy with yourself, just as you are.

Henry isn't afraid to be himself. In fact, he enjoys being himself. He remains honest and true to his feelings and everyone likes him for it.

"We may look different but we feel the same."

Milly Molly®

B O O K S

Other picture books in the Milly, Molly series include:

- Milly, Molly and Jimmy's Seeds — ISBN 1-86972-000-8
- Milly, Molly and Beefy — ISBN 1-86972-006-7
- Milly, Molly and Pet Day — ISBN 1-86972-004-0
- Milly, Molly and Oink — ISBN 1-86972-002-4
- Milly and Molly Go Camping — ISBN 1-86972-003-2
- Milly, Molly and Betelgeuse — ISBN 1-86972-005-9
- Milly, Molly and Taffy Bogle — ISBN 1-86972-001-6
- Milly, Molly and Alf — ISBN 1-86972-018-0
- Milly, Molly and Sock Heaven — ISBN 1-86972-015-6
- Milly, Molly and the Sunhat — ISBN 1-86972-016-4
- Milly, Molly and Special Friends — ISBN 1-86972-017-2
- Milly, Molly and Different Dads — ISBN 1-86972-019-9
- Milly, Molly and Aunt Maude — ISBN 1-86972-014-8
- Milly, Molly and Grandpa Friday — ISBN 1-86972-029-6
- Milly, Molly and the Secret Scarves — ISBN 1-86972-027-X
- Milly, Molly and the Stowaways — ISBN 1-86972-026-1
- Milly, Molly and the Tree Hut — ISBN 1-86972-028-8
- Milly, Molly and What Was That — ISBN 1-86972-031-8